The Scars We Don't See

micro-fiction by

Cassa Bassa

Raw Earth Ink

2023

First paperback edition May 2023

Edited by Candice Louisa Daquin

ISBN 978-1-960991-03-4 (paperback)

Published by Raw Earth Ink
PO Box 39332
Ninilchik, AK 99639
www.raw-earth-ink.com

*Dedicated to my son Ben,
and his late father Sean,
my mother Jing-Yun,
my father Xiang-Jie
and my partner Luca.*

"We write to taste life twice,
in the moment and in retrospect."
- *Anais Nin*

Table of Contents

Foreword

This isn't about me; it's about us.

That's the first feeling that came to mind when I started writing with Cassa. Instantly, there was comfortability in collaborating with her, an effortlessness, an appreciation, a wonder. There's a fearlessness I notice about the way she puts words to paper. And that is something that I can't help but admire.

If I remember correctly, I first came across her writing in early 2020—around Valentine's Day, in fact. And it's not an exaggeration when I say that I fell in love with her style at first sight. I connected deeply with the philosophical acumen, the spiritual presence, the genre-bending approach, the bold word choices, and varied subject matters. There is an unforgettable texture and substance behind her creations, no matter the medium or form they take on.

Within a few weeks we were writing together. (I think it was my idea.) And I'm glad she agreed because the process was instructive on many levels. Just seeing the way she works, with such focus and determination, with such imagination and playfulness was inspiring. We wrote numerous times afterwards, and hopefully we will again soon. Though what stands out for me the most was her unwavering spirit.

She is a true creative force, always pushing for the best possible outcome until the very end, and she never wavers in her artistic integrity. Yet another thing I admire about her, in a day and age where microwave art is all too common.

Through my own creative journey, I've been around a lot of

great writers. But I would put Cassa right at the top, because of the traits I mentioned above. In an imaginary scenario, if I ever needed someone to write a poem for me to save my life, I would choose her, since I respect her skill that much.

The first poem we ever wrote together was called "Wordsmith Apprentices". It's an interesting title because I never thought of Cassa as an apprentice. To me, she is as talented as they come in poetical endeavours, because she has the ability to entertain the reader, teach them without condescension, and make them feel something strongly. This kind of engagement is really important. But what stands out even more so... is Cassa's willingness to learn, improve, and strive toward better lines, better words, better stories.

About a year ago, when I was battling through a chronic illness, Cassa was one of the first people to contact me and offer support. Which showed me the kind of person she is, the kind of kindness she exudes, and it also showed me that she wasn't just a writing partner but a true friend. So, I'm glad this isn't about me, and it's about her.

Overall, it's really gratifying to read Cassa's work and see it in print. But it's even more gratifying to call her a friend.

I'm very proud of what she has accomplished, as an artist, daughter, mother, and human being. And forever and ever, I will think of her as a writing soulmate—as an inspiration.

Enjoy this wonderful book, which shows the depth of the human condition. I have faith that you will remember these words long after you've read the last page.

—Benjamin Grossman, author of *The Land Without Footprints*

Acknowledgments

This is my first published book. I thank God for reminding me of my dream of being a writer at the lowest point of my life.

I am grateful for my publisher tara caribou and editor Candice Louisa Daquin, without their guidance and professionalism, this book would not come together.

I would also like to thank Benjamin Grossman, David Mane, and Mike Ennenbach who encouraged me in my early writing journey.

I started my English writing on WordPress, where I met many talented and passionate writers from all around the globe. I am grateful for your support by reading and interacting with me. You have helped me to grow as a writer.

—Cassa Bassa

I See You

I make sense of the world around me,
the tales I hear, movies
or documentaries I watch,
by telling stories about the characters
I came to know.
That's how I process my inner conflicts
and try to make sense of it all.

Station

Grief brought winter rain to the city where his mother lay in peace.

She boarded the train with the intention of giving comforting hugs and perhaps running some errands to help.

To their surprise, she also brought the weather with her. Warm sun broke off the chill hanging in crisp air.

They both journeyed in a half-life to be in that exact moment, when their hearts finally embraced on that railway station platform.

"Life is the train and not the station" — Paulo Coelho.

Lotus

"The Lotus Award goes to Sage Holmes, CEO of the Detour House Women's Foundation." Her eyes well up in a room filled with standing ovations. She is wearing a white dress to receive this lifetime contribution award among a group of passionate servants who are just like her. Women who spend their lives tirelessly fighting for women's safety and providing a roof over their heads.

Thirty-three years ago, she was one of those women; without a voice, drug addicted and working in a brothel where she hardly saw any sunlight. There was this Salvation Army woman; a chubby kind woman, who always brought freshly baked cookies and would have a cup of tea and a chat with the girls. Her smile was bright, and her hugs were warm; she was *hope* and their only connection to the normality of the outside world.

"I am grateful for this acknowledgement, and I owe it to that Salvation Army woman who baked us cookies and always reminded us by saying: 'God made you girls like a lotus, living in mud but as pure as snow.' Thank you!"

Colour Extinction

Blue is one of the ancient colours found among turquoise, navy, and coral.

They belong to a group of natural colours once existing in abundance upon earth.

Many poets, painters, and song writers produced artistic renditions for centuries, inspired purely by these colours found in the natural world.

There used to be a major hydrosphere called an ocean which helped regulate the temperature across the globe.

Then the temperature of the earth continued to rise at an irreversible speed.

The result of that was the dry out of oceans and extinction of these related colours.

Surveillance

AFP agents were listening in to a pair of suspected criminals.

All they could hear seemed to be about domestic cleaning.

Agents were frantically decoding and reading between the lines.

The report read:
> 'It is the perfect strategy; to thoroughly clean up the nation's financial mess and progressively detoxify its people using abrasive ethnic cleansing.'

The pair stood in trial in High Court.

They were confronted with the sole evidence of live recordings of their bedroom conversation.

'The best way to clean up your home kitchen is to clean as you go, by using vinegar spray.'

*AFP = Australian Federal Police.

Life in Further Decline

He makes a living impersonating Elvis. Such talent gives him the means to feed a family of four; plus own two dogs and a tour van, which is also their humble mobile home. Living like gypsies, playing music, singing, and dancing by the fire under the Milky Way, is far from their reality.

Home-schooling and moving with tour schedules around small country towns have become 24/7 work with the reward of barely surviving. The real disaster comes when he no longer fits into the white Elvis jumpsuit with his middle-aged gut and overall puffiness from sleep deprivation.

What now? Is the question he pleads with his gods, while sewing up the buttons on his well-worn jumpsuit.

Scrap Metal

He was a written-off car, who didn't survive the crash. All the valuables and the brokenness were swept into the junk yard, waiting to be compressed into unidentifiable scrap.

His Maker has a habit of favouring scrap metals. He visits the junk yard often. In fact, He makes that a priority. He knows all metals by name, like He knows the stars.

When his Maker whispered his name, instantly he recognised Him. He knew exactly which precious metal he had been disregarding, how beaten up he was and how insignificant he felt. He responded, *"Here I am!"*

And that's all which was needed for him to be pulled out from the junk yard and joined with all other stars, to light up the glorious sky, once more.

A Lost Battle

The grinding sound of her own teeth woke her up. She moved her jaws and some saliva brought on a mild sweet taste. Her eyes gradually opened to the daylight piercing through the treetops. It's only just after ten, she checked her phone, no messages. This is normal for an unwanted waste of space.

She tried to get up from the hardwood park bench. Her neck and back aching. *The fucking methadone knocked me out again*, she cussed to herself. Her eyes met with a pair of doll eyes belonging to a toddler with curly hair. Her face suddenly got slapped by a thick little palm. *"Boo!"* the toddler uttered, covering her doll eyes with two tiny chubby hands. The hands ran down from the doll eyes to the nose, to the lips, smearing dribbles all over the face and the giggling doll eyes never left her face.

"Boo!" the little monkey called out again with upmost enthusiasm. She covered her eyes and called out peek-a-boo to the curly hair. This caused more giggles, rippling out onto the playground. The retiree moved in fast and took the hand of the doll eyes, pulling away from her. She saw the retiree's cautious fake smile. She gave back a fake smile and started walking out of the playground.

That was all too familiar to her. She knew she was clean and tidy these days. So, she could not have been mistaken to be a homeless outcast. Why then, did people still give her *the look*. Yes, *that* look. The fucking *not-sure-what-to-do* look. She thought it was the depressing aura of an unemployment benefit recipient that she was wearing. Everywhere she went, people stayed away. She saw through people. She knew she was not dumb; on the contrary, she was street smart. She ran the phone for her mum's strip party business in 6th grade. She had once had an adventurous life of stripping and travelling. If it wasn't for the heroin addiction, she would still be having that good life.

She got on a bus without a destination. Her daily luxury was the $2.50 flat rate pensioner's travel. She leaned her head to the window, looking out to a world she once belonged in. Watching school children waiting at the bus stop mucking around, she imagined her baby would be one of them, well-adjusted to this world. She was in two minds about trying to gain custody back. She had remained clean for almost two years, so she had a good chance to regain full custody. It had been a numb and lonely two years. She visited her local chemist daily to get her methadone doses. She was drugged up to her eyeballs every day. The only difference between methadone and heroin was she felt low all the time. If not fighting for the chance of being with her baby again, what would she have?

Now when the fighting was almost over, she felt the dread of not being able to dash across the finishing line. She felt so tired, so drained and so incapable of looking after herself, let alone a child. The fear of letting her baby down again, tormented her day and night. She was waiting to be judged as an incompetent mother and sentenced to a lonely low life, a constant living hell. She got off the bus and walked towards the scenic cliff walk. The blank state of her mind led her all the way to the cliff top where tourists were posing and taking selfies.

-- -- --

"Breaking news today, a Sydney ex-high-paid escort killed herself by jumping the Gap in front of a group of Japanese tourists close to noon. It is reported she has been fighting to regain the custody of her six-year-old son, who is under the foster care system. Cassandra reporting from the Five Network.

A Homeless Man

I have never seen such sallow vacant eyes.

They are the aftermath of a night's terror in a haunted house with rotting beams full of bats.

Even the early summer sun and warm breeze does not bring hope.

A lone scruffy man sits on a weathered park bench.

Crows are roaming around him, unearthing grubs.

I wonder if those park crows ever consider pecking him like they do with carrion.

Scarecrow

This is a story about a scarecrow and a farm helper.

The scarecrow was hand crafted by a farmer couple living in a village surrounded by rice paddies. They carefully created her with the late summer hay, natural dyed clothes, plaited straw hair, bamboo knitted hat, and brown marble eyes. She was as beautiful as a China doll.

The love the farmer couple poured into her made her the most precious scarecrow in the land. In return, she faithfully watched over the rice paddies throughout the seasons. She also watched the farmer couple tilling their land, planting, and harvesting crops together. She saw them sharing teas, meals, and sweets under the shady dancing willow. Oh, how she wished she could understand their smile and the way they looked at each other. She felt empty and sad because of her hollow heart.

In harvest seasons, the farmer couple hired a farm helper, an orphan boy from a village upstream. He had a good reputation in the land for being hardworking, respectful, and honest. Harvest was coming in a week. The helper returned to help prepare the tools and clearing the barns and storehouse.

The helper knew the scarecrow very well. They spent mealtime, rest breaks, and any free time the helper had together. The helper shared his daily happening with the scarecrow. Sometimes he told her his longing to know his parents and his sadness of being alone. The helper also played the harmonica at sunset especially for the scarecrow. The nostalgic sound of the harmonica saddened the scarecrow, but she was without speech so she could not express her feelings to him.

Every time the helper left the farm after the harvest season, he grew silent and gloomy because he missed the scarecrow terribly. He went on to work on other farms helping with building, feeding, and minding cattle, training farm dogs or anything which would make him a living. He read and played his harmonica in his spare time to help ease the pain of missing the scarecrow. He would also pass by the farmer couple's property regularly to see if they had any small jobs for him to do, so he could be with the scarecrow besides the spring and autumn harvests.

One day the farmer offered the helper a cook's position because his wife had fallen ill of a female problem which caused her to be weak and lethargic. The helper gladly accepted the offer and became the cook of the house. He not only performed diligently as the cook, but also managed the housekeeping of the farm. He spent his free time helping the farmer in the fields. Whenever he stopped to wipe off his sweat, he would look up at the scarecrow with a big grin, brighter than the morning sun. The farmers and the helper became great friends beyond the master and helper relationship.

Every spring and autumn, the helper lovingly strengthened and repaired the scarecrow using new hay. He made her different straw hats that matched the new outfits he sewed for her. The scarecrow always looked the best and remained the most victorious against all the birds to protect the farmers' rice crop.

The helper and the scarecrow faithfully served their duties for the farm and the land. They lived simply and adored each other in every way they could. If not for the scarecrow, the helper would have been a lone farmhand. If not for the helper, the scarecrow would have sadly watched over a land, eventually weather worn and devoured by birds.

Why Did You Run?

He needed to feed the parking metre before the concert finished, and he was busting to pee.

The clear option was a bathroom trip first, then feed the hungry box, but out of the corner of his eye, he saw the ranger looking at his number plate.

Shite! He couldn't afford to pay another fine.

Trying to beat the ranger to it, he raced towards his car.

The ranger looked up, her face turned ghostly pale and started to run.

He was puzzled, till he saw himself in the reflection of his car window, a six-foot-seven giant in a Kiss costume.

Lucky Strike

When Lucy grew up, the world was a lot different. Kids were allowed to buy cigarettes and alcohol in the local grocery stores, mostly for their parents and relatives.

Lucy used to skip down the street in her red plastic flip flops, tightly holding the money in her little hand; when she arrived at the grocery store, she reached her hand to the much taller counter and said, *"A pack of Lucky Strikes please"*.

The shopkeeper was curious to find out where the sound was coming from, as he could not see any customer in his store; *"A pack of Lucky Strikes please, for my Papa."* this time the little hand was waving a five-dollar note to attract the shopkeeper's attention.

"Ah, hello you, little one!"

"My Papa said five dollars to you and two dollars and seventy-five cents change for me."

"Your Papa is right, little one."

The shopkeeper took the five dollar note, handed back a pack of red Lucky Strikes and two dollars and seventy-five cents in change.

"Thank you, sir!"

"Oh wait, here is a sweet for you, for being such a good girl."

Red has been Lucy's favourite colour which reminds her of being a good girl in her red plastic flip flops, red Lucky Strikes in hand, and a raspberry red candy on her tongue. A sweet memory of her childhood.

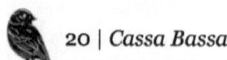

The Great Wall

If you ask me about the splendour of the Great Wall, I'd be too ashamed to admit that I have any connection to it. I would go so far to even deny that I am Chinese.

In 1997, Beijing's summer was hot and dry. After an unsatisfactory meal, I was dragged to go along to see the Great Wall. I couldn't think of anything worse to do. I would have been a lot happier to stay in the cheap hotel and enjoy a mouth-watering watermelon in air con.

The tourist bus took us all the way up to the top. People had already been queuing up to walk the Great Wall. I got off the bus, physically feeling sick. My stomach was churning, and I was about to throw up. My companions were in a dilemma. I saved their disappointment by excusing myself to the bathroom and asked them to go ahead to climb the Wall without me.

A bit of a breeze cooled my head. My stomach started to settle. I saw loads of people gradually disappearing like a snake crawling along the Great Wall. I sat on a chair in one of the stalls. The owner offered a service to write a poem based on my full name, on a banner with a Chinese calligraphy brush. I had some time to myself and was curious to see what he would come up with. In less than two minutes, he skilfully moved his brush and created a four-line poem with seven characters in each line. I was beyond impressed by his talent. His interpretation of my name gave a new meaning with blessings and depth.

I could not help but think that was my reward for not offending the ghosts by trampling their graves where the Great Wall had been laid upon. The Great Wall of China was built on human sweat, blood and lives, a place where the crows kept coming back for carcasses, buried long ago.

Deception

This time of the year, the splendid colour always reminds him of Clementine, a beautiful woman with porcelain freckled skin and fiery red hair.

She was neurotic, spontaneous, and wild. It was an instant attraction without reservation. He fell in love hard, like cedar wood.

How he wished that could be a fairy tale, ignoring her interchangeable sweetness and sourness. When he was around her, she blanketed him with warmth and zest. But when he embraced all she was giving out, there was always that invisible chill he felt. He was not a smart man. He only quit after seven broken hearts over three years.

Today, he still ponders about their love. This time of the year, in the forest of orange trees, he thinks about Clementine, a woman like the autumn cold air, whom he once loved deeply.

A Murderer's Mind

She was as slim as a cigarette.

He longed to be the filter between her divine lips.

Each smoke circle she oozed out blurred his vision and dizzied his mind.

He remembered what his Mama said to him; *'They came to steal your soul, son.'*

He pressed his hand firmly on her sexy mouth to muffle the screams till her eyes were wide open.

Eventually she was extinguished like a cigarette butt before being tossed into the dumpster.

Three Best Friends Forever

Julie sat, blank faced in silence, staring at the Japanese style crane wallpaper. Behind her, the gathering meal was being served. The service staff was pushing food carts. The sound of the wheels rolling across the wooden floor intersected with the footsteps of funeral guests.

"Jules... Jules... Julie!" Megan called out and placed her hand on Julie's bony shoulder. She was startled and broke out in a cold sweat. She instantly stood up and turned around. The crane wallpaper flew out of her vision and Megan's sleep deprived face gradually came into focus.

"Oh M!" she slumped herself into Megan's full busted chest. *"I am so glad that you are here. Oh my God! I need you. I can't believe Bella is gone."* She sobbed uncontrollably, the cries vibrating through her skin and bones.

"I am sorry I missed the whole service. I got here as soon as I could. I think I am still in shock that she is gone." Megan gently pressed Julie's head on her shoulder and comforted her with gentle patting on her back.

They stayed standing until she stopped crying. Megan took her hand and walked towards the courtyard. *"Tell me Jules, everything you know about what happened to Bella."*

They stood by the fence. Julie started chewing on her already bare nails. *"Oh M, it's a tragedy. I saw her last Sunday. We went to check out the new doggy grooming parlour in Westfield. And she missed the knitting class on Tuesday. I called and called."* Tears ran from her red swollen eyes.

"Johnny called me Wednesday morning and told me Bella is gone. She

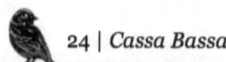

jumped the Gap Tuesday night, and the police search team found her body down the cliff. M, she is gone; it's too much for her. She couldn't do it anymore." She sobbed and hung onto Megan for comfort.

Megan was trying to absorb what Julie told her. In her mind, Bella's bright smile and the images of her and her adorable companion dog were playing like a film. *Bella jumped the Gap* was an unconceivable idea, let alone a piece of news that she had never prepared to receive. A surge of anger came up from her stomach to her throat. She let out a low grunt, quite out of her cool calm and collected character.

"I need a stiff drink, Jules, would you care for one, too?"

"I suppose it will do me good. Get me a White Russian, please."

Megan left Julie and walked straight to the bar where the funeral guests huddled and chatted in low voices. Megan ordered two White Russians and waited at the far side of the bar, where the screen shielded her from the rest of the crowd. She finally cupped her hands to her face and started to weep, then it turned into wailing. She felt a piece of her heart was stabbed and twisted by a serrated knife. She could barely breathe with her nose all congested and her head pounding.

Memories flooded back when they were struck together in the girl's refuge, a temporary home they shared. They had been damaged and traumatised by what had happened to them in their childhood and teenage years. They bonded immediately and became best friends forever.

They had their own demons to fight, but they always had each other to fight together through every outbreak and attack. Whenever Jules sank into an episode of anorexia nervosa, Bella and Megan took turns to take her to therapy and support groups, until she became stable again.

Megan tended to drown herself in work and alcohol, and she would lie to them about being busy and cut off contact. They would knock at her apartment door and bring popcorn for a girl's night in, which often worked as an intervention to avoid her going into a downward spiral.

Bella seemed to be the well-adjusted one. She was giving, loving and the only one who managed to have a proper relationship. Even after she had that silent miscarriage, instead of wallowing in sorrow, she took up knitting classes to learn how to make Care Bears for the hospital where she stayed. There was no clue that she would end her own life, absolutely no clue.

Megan thought to herself, *Even Bella could not endure the pain of her past, will I be next?*

God's Plan

The day the Premier passed the bill, granting him unprecedented power, the people who fought for their freedom felt downtrodden and devastated. The political climate cast a blanket of dark clouds over the state. Every day ordinary people, fell ill, foreseeing tyrannical days ahead.

There was a group of people who went up to the highest place of the city and wept bitterly to their God. The mountain shook, and soon after, a hailstorm broke out. They fled to seek refuge under some banana plantation.

When all was passed, they heard of the news that their Premier was struck dead by an enormous hailstone while giving a celebratory speech at a press conference outside the parliament house.

Con

He shops around on dating sites. From an early banter, it progresses into a coffee date, a small token to test out the potential of such an investment. He does it diligently every week like Sunday mass, till he shortlists a few.

Commitment is not his plan. He hovers over a few lovers like watching the stock market. The only difference is he is doing it without any financial investment. He merely used what is given to him by one victim to lure another in for greater profit.

Chester Gallery

The night made its way into the depth of darkness.

In the dim light of a kerosene lamp, he plaited the coarse strands into resilient strings with his nimble fingers.

He fervently stretched the anaemically pale canvas onto the frame.

Shades of red mixed in an aesthetic colour palette; he restored each painting with precise brush strokes.

When the twilight arrived, he hung all the art works back and marvelled at his resurrection.

Curator Chester Gallery was arrested on 13th September 1888 for the serial murders of art students in the gallery where he worked.

A Labour of Love

When Sage was a young girl, she applied the theory of love to her life. Soon she discovered that love was a multi-faceted gemstone. Love didn't just shine on its own.

Sage learned the patience of mastering her craftsmanship. Through trial and error, she progressively coaxed love out, to be shining bright.

The love Sage laboured over became the most precious gemstone in heaven.

Keepsake

There was a poet living in poverty. His only possession was his words.

He was secretly in love with the shoemaker's daughter. So, every day he wrote a love poem and whispered to her as a keepsake.

She was born tender-eyed and was not married, even way past childbearing age. But all the days of her life, she was happy, especially when she saw how beautiful she was in the mirror.

Falling Apart

Their ten-year-old boy is dying of leukaemia. He is looking sick and pale.

They decided to put aside their differences and take him to sunny Noosa for a family holiday. It is a huge commitment because they have been living completely separate lives since their divorce five years ago.

The weather has been lovely until they arrive at the beach villa which is overlooking the stormy ocean. Not sure if it's the exhausting long drive and emotions, or the contrast between the rambunctious waves and their departing child, they broke down and sobbed uncontrollably, together.

Silence Speaks Volumes

She married a much older man in Tasmania in exchange for a better life for her family in a small village in Thailand. He was reserved and quiet but treated her with respect.

There was little verbal communication between them because of the language barrier. They went everywhere and did everything together, until he fell ill approaching the sunset of his life.

She stayed by his side and nursed him till he let out his final breath in peace. Their rather silent life spoke volumes in mutual love and respect.

Paradox

It has always been easy for Sage to make connections with strangers. She feels they are all related somehow in the vast Cosmos. Her heart is an open door for the sharing of stories.

There is no surprise to see Sage giving an inspiring speech in a high society fund raising ball, sharing a coffee and cigarette with a homeless sister on a street corner, or taking her elderly neighbour to her Aqua therapy every Monday afternoon.

But in her household, she was given the cold shoulder for her career success by the one who should have supported her, criticised for her strict discipline by her children, and misunderstood for her tireless giving, thought to be personal ambition.

Sage sheds tears in her prayer room for the unity she so strives for, but it doesn't seem to be any closer in her own backyard.

The Poet and One of His Readers

He escapes from the everyday reality to immerse himself in aged books. The fragrance between the crispy vintage pages infuses his nostrils like April blooms. He imagines someone is reading one of his poems under a flaming Japanese maple bathed in autumn glory.

She shies away from the crowded room and retreats into the oversized recliner in the studies; letting the scent of old poetry books calm her mind. Her delicate fingers dance with each stanza in rhythms only Braille can play so fluidly. She wonders how his hand moved when he composed all those crests and troughs so pleasing to her heart.

Post Trauma

The farmers survived the calamity of the bushfire. They ran out of adrenaline. What they must face now, is the remnant of destruction.

The ground is covered with green again, but they still smell char. It's both painful to hear people talking about the fire and stop talking about the fire. The farmers are desperately trying to get on with their lives, to smile at each other with desolate eyes.

The Curse

My feet are numb, and my hands slowly come into focus. I see my stiffened crooked fingers. I don't have arthritis. I use my thumbs to run over my fingertips. The sticky and slimy texture sends chills to my rib cage. I feel the need to pee desperately. My body starts shivering in convulsions with the sensation of rain slapping on me.

*Shhhh-tik-tik-tik…Shhhh-tik-tik-tik…*The sound of the lawn sprinkler draws me to an awakening state. Relying on the moonlight, I find myself standing in my backyard soaked in my pyjamas. It is July, in the middle of winter, Sydney's temperature drops to 4°C. I raise my hands in front of my eyes. I see a red stain trickling down to my elbows. *"Aaaaah!"* I let out a shriek.

The garden light comes on. The next thing I know is that I slump into my father's arms shaking uncontrollably.

"Katie! Katie! Sweetheart, shh…shh…You are home safe, darling."

"Daddy, do you see the blood? I don't know what's wrong with me." I am sobbing in fear and hyperventilating. I stare at my own hands, which aren't my hands.

"Darling, you are having nightmares again. That's all. Shh…shh…You are safe."

"It's not a nightmare Daddy. I was standing on the lawn. I saw myself with gnarled fingers just like the curse. It is real, Daddy. They are coming for me to repay the lives I took."

"Baby, it's untrue. They are just bluffing. There is no proof for it. It's some kind of dark magic or spell they cast on you. You are innocent. You are my angel. There is no way you took any life. You hear me, Katie? That is a lie!"

The Middle Class 'Struggle'

She popped open a chilled bottle and sculled* down an overflowing glass of bubbly to calm the adrenaline rush she got after making expensive purchases.

It's 2:30pm. Soon she would need to pick up the kids from school. She hurried down to the basement with bags of luxury fashion items from Madison Avenue and stuffed them in the empty archive boxes. On her way out to do the school run, she intercepted the mail addressed to her from debt collection companies.

She had been waiting anxiously till the front door opened when the clock had just struck 8pm. His presence gave her great relief for another week of pay cheques to maintain their facade.

*Sculled = drink it all in one go (Australian saying).

70's Wedding Blues

I remember the day of your wedding. Pear blossoms paved the way from your bedroom to the village gate. The red of your wedding gown was the only symbol of happiness in a time when the entire village barely survived the famine.

The groom didn't come with any pig or buffalo as dowry. You were married out to reduce a mouth that needed feeding.

The rusty tractor took the newlyweds away, disappearing deeper into the mountains and left a trail of mud from the spring rain wrestling with the firecrackers. The elders said your marriage started off on a rough path already.

<u>Chopper</u>

Life dealt him a bad hand that no child should have had to withstand. A broken soul became a hardened man who experienced neither pleasure nor pain in the act of violence.

Prison life gave him a chance to be a vigilante who enacted justice for abused and murdered children.

He thought about the Boss upstairs a lot. He thought to himself *'I am only an eye for an eye, a tooth for a tooth. I will make it to heaven. My life isn't such a bad deal after all.'*

Tom

It's the neighbourhood gardening day.

Tom blushed when she handed him pine straws to put on the topsoil of the roses. Electricity passed through from her pale fingers to his knuckles. No one noticed any strangeness in his raw red face because they thought he was just bothered by the heat. She offered him a cold drink, homemade lemonade. He gladly accepted it for another chance to be electrified by her womanly touch. He swallowed the drink hard, feeling the contracting movement of his own throat. Thank God for the cold lemonade to put out some fire.

She rested one leg up on a garden chair, dusting some dirt off her shoe. She looked up and smiled at him while switching to the other leg. Tom was instantly overcome by a warm gush in his crotch. He ran straight back towards his house, almost knocking down his mother.

He locked his bedroom door, pulled the curtain shut and dropped his pants. He masturbated almost violently with the flashing images of her angling her leg in front of her bathroom mirror and shaving delicately between her thighs. The second waves hit him soon after. He was swept away by the combination of heat exhaustion and orgasmic pleasure. Then came the shame of being a teenage boy peeping on his neighbour, who is his mother's age.

Scars We Don't See

"Morning ma'am, what can I offer you today"? I paused; you looked familiar. I recognised the scar across your forehead and the missing front tooth when you squeezed out a smile.

"You don't recognise me? Cindy! My name is Cindy. The Neighbourhood Centre found us a unit and I scrubbed up."

"Oh Cin! O-M-G! I didn't recognise you. You... you look good, Cin." It dawned on me that you were the homeless lady who had hung around my cafe with two kids; a boy and a girl.

"Let me make you a coffee. What would you like? My shout to celebrate, you got a home now. That's a big deal."

"Oh no, Patricia, thanks for the offer. I won't take up your time. Just wanna see if you need a helper in the kitchen? Like unloading deliveries, washing dishes, taking the trash out? I, ah, I can't do the front house duties 'cause of my tooth... My kids are going to school now, just around the corner. They can walk to school by themselves. I got free time to work, and I can do with some money to get some stuff for the unit."

"Uhm, look Cin, I don't really need any helper's 'cause my older boy is doing the kitchen hand stuff." I thought about it some more. *"But he got into uni, it's starting soon. How about you come in tomorrow at noon to do a work trial, and I'll cut him a bit of slack. I'm sure he'd be happy to hang out with his mates."*

"Oh, sure, sure...thank you sooo much. I'll be here before twelve tomorrow. You're an angel, Patricia." You cupped your hands to your face and almost shouted in your excitement.

"That's alright, Cin...and call me Trish. Patricia is just a bit formal you know," I laughed and winked.

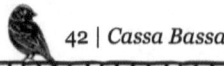

"Okay, okay Trish, boss lady!" You chuckled with your hand covering your mouth to hide the missing tooth.

You came almost half an hour before midday in the same white shirt and black pants you wore yesterday. The cafe was quite busy with almost all the tables needing clearing from the mid-morning rush. You dived straight in, taking empty plates, cups and cutlery to the kitchen and came back with an apron on, to spray and wipe down the tables. You kept your head down, avoiding eye contact with the customers leaving the cafe. You worked swiftly, and I was thankful that you turned up early.

First day of your work trial, you did good, with only a moment or two of spacing out. I attributed it to you being out of work for a long time, figuring it might take some time to readjust. I asked you to come back the next day but didn't promise a regular job. Being a small business owner and a single mother, I had learned to put my little family first and not make promises that I couldn't keep.

The third day of the work trial came. In reality, I needed someone who could do the front and the back of the cafe. But I knew what this job would mean to you as a mother, and to your finances. I was contemplating offering you 11am to 2pm shifts on weekdays. That would cover some food prep and cleaning up for the lunch rush which would free up me and the two other girls for customer service and the till. I was going to tell you at the end of the day.

Then it happened. I saw you spacing out in the middle of slicing mushrooms, then you were pacing around the kitchen and the chef had to stop in the middle of cooking some sauce to ask if you were okay. It took you a while to snap back to reality. You walked back to the bench and kept slicing mushrooms. I was taken aback by what I saw. Call it a woman's instinct; I knew something was wrong with you neurologically.

I took you outside to get some fresh air. I wasn't going to give you some lame excuse for not offering you a job. I told you straight up about my concerns. I figured I owed you that basic decency. You opened up to me and told me drugs and alcohol abuse had damaged your brain. Even though you had been drug- and alcohol-free for a good while, the damage was done from teenage years and was irrevocable.

I hugged you and cried. The scar you carried on your forehead or the missing tooth was just the damage people saw. The damage inside was a lot more profound.

Part 1 – Ankle Bracelet

Your scent infused me before you sat next to me. A rose blossom wrapped in leather; you slid into the oversized executive chair next to me in the boardroom. My brain kept telling me to focus on the presenter and the screen, battling my distracted mind and wandering eye. I pushed my chair backward, so I had a better view of you, such a challenger to my professionalism. My eyes fixated on the rose gold ankle bracelet you wore, set with onyx stone and pavé diamonds. It was such a sexy playful little thing.

Not all office romances start the same and not all love affairs end in tragedy. I am a stockbroker. I gamble, with calculated risk of course. *'The winner takes it all.'*

Part 2 – Aura of Mystery

Who are you? I need to know as much as possible about you so I can have a winning strategy.

The aura you wear is of mystery. You look sweet but dressed to kill. You smell of wild sex, but you put an invisible barrier between us while we are only ten metres apart in this more crowded than usual boardroom. I can't quite work you out, yet.

The ankle bracelet. I wonder if your toes are manicured and painted red or black? When you run your toes around me, will the bracelet be a distraction?

Focus, Tommy! I snap myself out of the trance you put me in. Clearing my throat, I swallow and force my attention to the line graph on the presentation screen.

Part 3 – The Kissing Song

"Now let's invite our next guest speaker, Ami Sickle from SAFAA to talk about the upcoming professional development opportunities and the annual conference."

Ami! Your name is Ami.
Tommy and Ami Sitting in a tree
K-I-S-S-I-N-G!
First comes love
Then comes marriage
Then comes baby
In a baby carriage!

You are standing in front of me without any obstruction, giving a presentation. It's gonna be a full cinematic experience.

Ami Sickle, your dark hair wraps around your fair neck on one side, rose pink pouting lips, somewhat comfortable in your petite hugging knee high black dress, black heels, huh, and the rose gold ankle bracelet in between. Ami, you are sexy and cute. I'm gonna have a lot of fun with you. I can feel my cheeks smiling.

"Hi guys! I am Ami, Marketing Executive from The Stockbrokers and Financial Advisers Association. Today, I am presenting…"

Your voice stills me. It's like the zither being played by the waterfall, calming and Zen. The fantasy of pinning you to the wall and pleasuring you from behind dissipates. I thought I worked you out, but I am not so sure now. Who are you, Ami Sickle?

Part 4 – Self Nomination

I stop you on your way out of the boardroom door.

"Ami, I am Tommy, Tommy Lee. Do you want to grab a bite to eat in the city after work today?"

You look at me and smile. Oh Ami Sickle, I love your dimples! They look like a pool of happiness, so overwhelmingly sweet and beautiful!

"Hey, Tommy! I am not available. Thank you!"

"How about some time this week...or beyond? You are gonna be hungry one of these days?"

"Ah, Tommy, what I meant was I'd like to keep a professional boundary. I won't be grabbing a bite to eat with you. See you at the annual conference, if you are attending."

You just said no to me. Was it a 'no: try harder'? Or a 'no: NO'? *"Do you need a volunteer to help with organising the conference? I can help wherever you need me. I am a good helper."* What? Tommy! You just nominated yourself to work for free? The *Return on Investment* is so low considering the time and effort I must put in. Fuck! What's wrong with you?

"Ah, the conference is well-funded; it's not run by volunteers. And I don't think I need volunteers. But I appreciate your willingness to get involved and help. By saying that though, Tommy, I am still unavailable."

What? Did you just give me a hard NO? You are not willing to give me any bit of you. There must be another move I can make. Think, Tommy! I can't fucking think, it's like the market is closed today. I have to wait for tomorrow. But I don't want to wait and there is no other way. Am I throwing a tanty*? Shame on you Tommy, you're gonna accept defeat, aren't you?

"Tommy, there is this retirement village I volunteer at, they are really short of volunteers, and I know they will appreciate some help. I can email you the details and perhaps you can think about it?"

Oh Ami, you must have noticed that I looked defeated. You have a soft and kind heart. How can I not say yes, and I have to restrain myself from jumping for joy. You have just kept the door of hope ajar.

*Tanty = tantrum (Australian slang)

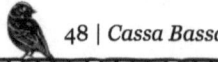

Seasons

She knows all the seasons from the bottom of the well.

The fragrant rain of red and white Ruby Cascade drizzles in springtime.

Her skin is covered with mosquito bites all through summer.

She hears the honeyeaters singing and imagines them hovering whilst feeding off the Grevillea.

When the bats start returning to share the well, she knows it is wintertime.

If you have been held captive in a well for seven years, you would learn to notice all seasons without counting the days.

Tiger Lily

The humid Colombia heat wakes her up from the drug induced slumber. Her sundress is lifted by the Caribbean Sea breeze, revealing bronzed legs.

Drifting higher, the breeze exposes bruises, signs of the kind of *'love'* she receives from the one who keeps her there. But she has become strong and hardened like clay in the hot sun.

She calls out to her pet leopard; *"Come here, my little one."* It pounces on her playfully, causing her to let out a string of laughter like a wind chime. *"Let's go swimming, okay?"*

She slips out of her dress and runs toward the sea with her best friend, the leopard named 'Congo.'

He frees up his hand from the cigar and claps, watching his gorgeous, prized prey bounding off toward the sea with her reward, Congo, for being such a good girl. He makes loads of connections with other drug lords simply by having her on his arm.

He can't bear it any longer, seeing her soft body in the ocean water. He makes his way down with that bullying grin on his face while unbuttoning his chino shorts. He can't wait to pin her down in the salty water and make her submit to his authority.

She hates being his captive. But then again, he is the only love she ever knew since she was twelve. Even the first to take her flower, which is why he named her Tiger Lily, after his favourite flower, exotic and wild. She will happily be his, until her youth runs out, if he doesn't make her spend endless nights entertaining his business partners. Those monsters are into some sexual deviances that leave scars on her body and soul.

Already strongly erect, and strutting like a rooster approaching her. Once he reaches her, he grabs the back of her head and violently pushes her down to his crotch under the saltwater. The more she struggles to breathe and fight back, the more his urge gets satisfied. In his twisted mind, he recalls her angelic face when he first laid eyes on her, her body was just starting to develop. Now, she is like a leech to him. He feeds her food, alcohol and drugs. She will do anything to keep herself fed and alive. He wants to think that she is a treasure because her divine body brings business to his kingdom. But the image of her being a sex slave in an orgy infuriates him. How could an angel become such a dirty slut? His anger wilts him instantly. He pulls her up and throws her into the sea as far as his rage allows. He spits into the water while he stumbles back to shore, hissing and cussing.

Tiger Lily feels a sense of great relief that he turns his back. She is so used to his violent outbursts; she doesn't think much of it. She knows how to keep herself alive. And now is the perfect opportunity. She swims further out towards the rocks with Congo leading the way. They did many practice swims at night on this route, so without much effort, they arrived at a small shore just behind the rocks which is the only spot invisible to their surveillance. She rises from the sea like a mermaid, her skin is glistening. *"Baby,"* she throws herself to her lover's broad chest and kisses him passionately. Congo is sitting next to the pair, keeping watch. He reluctantly pulls her away and puts a t-shirt over her, then rushes them to jump on the speed boat. He accelerates to the highest speed, disappearing to the island where they will board a cruise to Costa Rica.

At nightfall, Tiger Lily, her lover, and Congo arrive at the secluded bungalow he arranged for her escape. Excited and exhausted, he fixes some fresh meat for Congo, so the creature settles on the deck overlooking San Andrés. Now he is all hers.

She sits at the low end of the steps leading to the beach, her chin to her knees tucked underneath his oversized white t-shirt, her chestnut hair swept to the side. He walks over to her with a glass of chilled fresh coconut juice, kisses land gently on her burned skin where the t-shirt doesn't cover. *"Come sit with me, babe."* She links her arm with his and rests her head on his shoulder without another word. They hold such silence in absolute harmony until the stars blanket the sable sky. *"Let's go get some rest, my beautiful mermaid. We'll be home soon."* He scoops her up in his strong arms and carries her back into the bungalow. She loops her arms around his neck and stares deep into his emerald eyes. *"You are my home."*

Hole in the Wall

Tourists from all over the world come to this place to sight-see the old ruin and the ancient city as well as experience one of the richest cultures. The modern city is built on the wealth generated from the tourism and hospitality industries. This place never sleeps and is filled with alluring activities all year round.

He climbs over the old city gate with his makeshift sleeping bag and settles in a hole of his choice for the night in the old city wall. It doesn't take long for him to drift off, feeling cosy in his shelter, with the celebratory music vibrating from the modern city through to the old city walls. He lives in the gap of the ancient ghosts and the modern slaves.

Why Didn't I Call

Arash is the son of Persian immigrants from Iran. He is a Mechanical Engineer from Sydney. Since the 2014 Martin Place terrorist attack, he has become the subject of high security alerts during his work travels. His backyard backs on to the national park where the body was discovered.

"Detective, uhm... I didn't want to be the one to report a body near the vicinity of my backyard. I checked to make sure she was dead. If she had any sign of life, I would have called an ambulance straight away. I thought someone else would find her and report to the police. I ah...look at me! I just didn't want to be an Arab reporting a murder. I am over being stopped and searched at the customs because of my appearance. I am an Australian, you know! Anyway. Maybe I just watched too many crime series. I am sorry. I should have called you guys. My God, the poor woman."

A *Little bit* of Me & a Whole Lot of *Fiction*

These stories are largely fictional,
but you will also see fragments of me.

I Am Me

I am me and I am always just me. Please don't get hung up by pronouns. It's just one of the ways the world shows its craziness.

I have a preferred name which I respond to with a smile when called. If you are confused when you see me on paper or a screen, that's okay. I like that my name evokes childlike curiosity in you. Ask away! I am stoked that you are interested in getting to know me.

Please be at ease when you converse with me. You will never offend me if you open your heart and make your love available to me, just like I am to you. No question is a silly one when it comes from a genuine loving heart.

I am me and I am always just me.

Bend

Sometimes it is difficult to tell a story without admitting I am a slow learner in life's lessons.

My determination and commitment to love didn't lead me to *happy ever after*. Instead, it triggered a series of unfortunate love affairs which I was blindsided by, despite my faith in the necessity of having a strong will.

And by the same strong will, I have not given up on love. With the same diligence, I have found myself like a donkey pulling a mill, keep pressing on bit by bit, till I pass the bend. There will be a day when I see the harvest of believing in things unseen.

Little Girl in a Big City

The tired city is as exhausting as the social media feed. It loses its stimulus. The influence it possesses to empower and be impulsive. The anxious feeling holds her in a spinning fidget. Everywhere her sight is exposed to, sends a chilling spasm to her core.

Who would think under the city limelight, there are souls feeling so drained and distained? She wonders if she is trapped in a mortal body with a timeless soul. Layers and folds of wrinkled psyche that are unable to stay afloat.

There is no mirror on the wall to tell her future, neither a fantasy bubble floating in the suffocating air to give a glimpse of hope. She can only pick at her scars to remind herself that she was once alive and loved. Pain used to be her lover, who now has long gone. Numbness invaded her every cell. She wonders if she will be the sole witness of her own diminishment. Will the sleeping world even notice if the stars blink out, one by one?

The Selfish Writer

She woke up in the middle of the night. He was smoking weed, tripping, and reading a book.

We need to break up, she said, *I am breaking up with you.*

What? Why? What's going on babe?

I am a writer, and I can't write without feeling things, I haven't been feeling it since I met you.

But baby, how can that be my fault? I haven't done anything wrong, he protested.

Shut up and fuck me to oblivion, my head hurts.

He obliged. She is his sin and everything is about her.

The Promise Ring

You are so far away from me now.

If not for your long shadow, I wouldn't have remembered us.

All our past was edited into this novel for someone out there to read.

My bookshelves are filled with read books, except this one.

The Coke can pull-tab bookmarked the page where you proposed to me with that promise ring.

The innocence of pure love stopped me from reading the rest of the tragedy.

Centrifugation

We used to think of our future as retirees.

You would be content to tie our boat to the pier at sunset, with or without fish for dinner, while I would dream that you played the harmonica in nostalgic tunes by the sea.

We wanted simple things, until we didn't want them anymore, unintentionally.

There had been this period of vacant time, spinning too fast and too wild.

We lost hold of each other, and we lost our substance as one.

I often imagine, the day I learn to forget the past, and you learn to play the harmonica, we will share coffees together like two perfect strangers, who fall in love all over again.

The Girl in the Wardrobe

The sound of the wardrobe door closing is the best sound in the whole wide world. The wardrobe is like a hedge keeping the outside noise away. Mum's endless sighing, sometimes sobbing... Dad's jokes that only his drunk friends would laugh at, and his limited praising phases: *"That's my girl... you are smarter than your mum or I can tally up,"* or shouting: *"What the fuck is wrong with the internet now.... fuck this Copper Wi-Fi shit!"*

Before we moved into this house, I had to screen out these noises by playing hip-hop or house music with my earphones on. I felt my hearing was declining. My school friends told me I couldn't hear them most of the time. I had headaches sometimes because of so much noise.

This house is great; it is only a rental, but it is heaps better than the house we had before, solely because of this full-length wardrobe. It smells of wood and feels grainy. When I close the door, it muffles the world a bit and it is so quiet. I finally remove the earphones and stop playing music. I read, write, draw, and play on my tablet.

Winter vacation is coming. I am so excited because I can spend more time tucked away in the wardrobe. I have prepared a blanket and a cushion so I can even take my nap in this secret world of mine. Oh, I also pulled out the reading lamp from the storage. It's one of those rechargeable lamps with a clipped end. I envision myself reading under the warm light after dinner on a cold winter evening.

The trashy TV sound, the storm created by human beings, the agony caused by unhappy marriage and unemployment, are all shut out by this squeaky timber wardrobe door. That is how my childhood will be preserved. I am determined that as long as I have my sanctuary in this wardrobe, I will grow up to be happy.

In Your World

I am dreading the walk down the long sterile corridor leading to your room, which looks extra clinical today.

There is only duty left, rather than of any maternal attachment, for which I am here every week to see you.

I am a bit envious that you don't remember my name; you don't hold me in your arms like you used to; but you stroke the plush cat I brought in with me, like you used to with the family ginger cat.

I don't understand the world you are living in, Mama. You are talking to a toy cat like you always did in front of my teary eyes, and yet you are so far away from me.

Second Best

There were three people in that relationship. He probably didn't realise, but she was acutely aware from day one. She had learned to trust her instincts, which was a God-given gift.

Love is a complicated thing as much as it is plain and simple. There was no room for three. She didn't plan on showing up in his life to serve as a *pick-me-up* because he was toyed around by his goddess who he worshipped endlessly. The elusive and maybe-one-day possibility hung in his mind and their newfound relationship.

Love is a beautiful thing. It can make you forget any sadness and insufficiencies. But time is a cruel reminder. Any newness and rawness eventually wore off. Old habits and feelings crept back in. After all, she was his second best. She couldn't work out what happened and what changed.

Love is fragile, and it breaks so easily. A slip from a careless hand, a snuffle by unexplainable silence, or a hesitation that lasted a little too long, all shattered into pieces simultaneously. It was a sad reality really, no one came out unharmed from that crowded room, even it was only in their minds. Our minds set us free as much as imprison us. She chose to fly far away from their love maze and wanted no part in it for her own self-preservation, and time showed her that her instincts were right all along.

Fly, Fly Away

When I was little, I loved dragonflies. I lay still by the riverbank and waited for them to land on me. And they did: on the hem of my skirt, on my hair. I was amazed by how trusting they were.

Then there were boys who chased them away from me. I tried to turn up at the riverbank at different times of the day, so the boys could not find me. But they always did. They brought roasted peanuts and threw shells at me, sometimes cow dung. I wasn't bothered by their attacks because I knew that's the way boys showed interest. I was annoyed by their disturbance of my special time with the dragonflies.

One day I told my uncle that the boys threw peanut shells and cow dung at me by the riverbank. He started to take the buffalo for a wash in the river in mid-mornings, and my aunties washed their clothes in the afternoons in the river.

I reunited with the dragonflies in peace and tranquillity. And that was the highlight of my summer holidays at my grandparents' farm aside from sliding down the banana tree and ripping my skirt to shreds, but that is another story, for another time.

Hindrance

I heard that you had been back to visit the old town where we grew up and shared our first secret. It has been years since I counted the seasons, where the pear blossoms covered the laneway to our sweet youth. You always picked the snow-white blossoms out of my hair, and I always searched for your soul in your dark eyes. Time was an oblique concept back then. We were never hurried to grow up while we were glued to each other. The southern biting cold was our excuse to be touching skin and mingling our breaths. I still remember the sweet green apple taste of your mouth.

I haven't been back for years, probably since the day of your wedding. All I remember was my world came to an end that day. I can't remember how I managed to sweep up my broken heart and keep going, how I made it to the city, how I started to be a different version of myself, who remains a stranger to this day. People say love hurts.

The train is coming in eleven minutes. I need to get on this train to make it to grandma's funeral. For the first eighteen years of my life, grandma was my rock and my shelter. I failed to visit her all these twenty years and missed the chance to say goodbye. For that, I hate you. I hate your careless decision and it robs me of the ability to keep loving. This hurts, it really hurts. It hurts so much that I must step out of my own body to avoid the pain.

The clock on the platform is counting down. I see a grown woman sitting alone sobbing. Her face is contorted by grief or pain; I can't differentiate which. She looks so small and helpless. The door opens. I get on the train and sit by the window, keep on watching her. Soon she is fading into only a smudge. I wonder what is stopping her from boarding this train, and why she is so sad.

On My Mind

I long to be far away with my thoughts on a long-stretched highway between tall pines breaking apart into yellow and ultramarine blue. I appreciate beauty in all its primary forms. I don't ever feel that I fall short of my own shadow when light is all there is to tell a different story.

I didn't want to let go of my father's old Ford Thunderbird, because I still get excited about each time my long scarf flies through the sunroof, the accidental freedom, the sensation of unexpected wonder, and the unbidden joy.

I'd like to hold on to these long drives all the way to the top of the lookout, where your name always echoes deep in the Blue Mountains. The pine needles snow down in yellow and ultramarine blue flakes. When they land on the bottom of the mountain range, sometimes they pool into tranquil green and sometimes sorrowful hazel.

An Old Friend

An old friend came to haunt me last night in my restlessness.

He laughed that sarcastic laugh, and his words pierced my facade *"You are not happy, are you? Even though you have the world, you are still unhappy. You are incapable of being happy."*

It's true, my friend. I have come to terms with it. I am just a miserable woman who can't seem to be content and satisfied with what she has.

There was once a door I kept open to let the liar and accuser in. He became an old friend who is unwilling to leave without destruction, and I have been accustomed to that friendship.

Books

Books are a safe place to hide. The avalanche of emotions expressed in everybody's but my own story.

I have the whole world in my reading room. It is vast enough, so I burn my suitcase into ashes. Who cares if I don't set foot out of this door again?

Books hold me hostage to the freedom I always hope to find in them.

Alive

She was numb and dead inside. The forced rest in the asylum hadn't helped. With sedatives, the night terrors stopped, but she increasingly disassociated from her surroundings. The most frightening aspect was that she could no longer feel the warmth of the sun.

In a night like any other night, she was woken up by an owl. She responded to the owl's calling, escaping the night guard's watch. In her night gown and bare feet, she followed the line of the tall pencil pines, passing the mossy garden door. It was in late autumn, but she felt no cold.

When she was deep into the bush, the moon was high and bright, but the lake was dark and dead. She saw the owl on the tree branch watching her. The owl made another call. This time, she followed the sound and looked over to the lake again. She saw flecks of silver, then a fish jumping high above the water, then a few fish followed.

Her heart leaped and started thumping. She turned to the owl, and it was gone. Instead, there were two possums chasing each other on the branch, the tree leaves, making rustling sounds. She lay on the ground covered with dry leaves; they crackled like popcorn.

She heard the earth breathing steadily underneath her. She kept watching the possums and smiled at the moon every now and then. She hadn't felt so alive for a very long time.

Banyan

The banyan trees watch generations like the gods in the temple. The incense and burnt offerings keep their worship worthy.

They take me back to my childhood when I followed my great grandmother into the temple and knelt next to her. I mimicked her by bowing down. Our foreheads were touching the ground. I heard her pleading with the gods to take off twenty years of her own life and give it to my sick aunty. I cried. Silently, I asked the gods to be generous and to give both my aunty and my great grandmother a long life.

I know my prayer was answered by God. My great grandmother lived to ninety-seven with very little health complaints. My aunty is in her sixties. The banyan trees were my witness.

God hears our desperate cry, even in a temple filled with idols which he hates.

Different Sound

The city became so unbearable, she finally moved to the suburbs where greenery filled her eyes.

She woke up to some pleasing sound, different from the noise of the city traffic or people's small talk. It was sound of competition and harmony interchanging among the trees.

She lit a cigarette, but it felt offensive to smoke it. She felt the same with takeaway meals.

Living only with the company of birds made her realise there was so much junk in her life that she could better live without.

Goodbye Mum! Hi Mum!

I couldn't find many family photos with Mum in it, to put into the slide show for her celebration of life service. There were plenty of photos of me with Dad and other family members.

That summed up how I felt about Mum. She wasn't in my life that much. It was Dad took me to school on my first day, and she managed to miss almost all my significant firsts.

I held such belief until the day of her funeral. A relative of ours gave me a hug when she arrived at the service. She said to me with teary eyes, *'I am gonna miss your mother, she was always been there for everyone and made herself invisible.'*

Throughout the service, I heard Mum's friends and family members telling stories of their fond memories of Mum. In their minds, Mum was this selfless woman who always shied away from the crowd, just like the photos. She ran around to snap memories and hid behind the camera.

It dawned on me that she did the same with me. She worked hard and provided for our family and barely took any credit for that. I would prefer her to be a mummy bear, to nurture me. Instead, she was a lone eagle. I realised how much she had shielded me. I was just too frightened to look up to her when she soared above the storm of life.

The Art of Life

It took a lifetime to sketch our love story.

There is magic in this old medium, where beauty crafted from painstaking attention.

It would be ideal if we recorded our first encounter and played it back when we wanted to walk away from each other.

If we could make a copy of our honeymoon and broadcast it throughout our hardships, it would have been an easier journey.

Video held old memories as new, we wanted to believe.

But after a lifetime of creation, our story became a piece of intriguing art.

It's Gonna Be Okay

She sits in her grandma's rocking chair crocheting the blanket she started but was too frail to finish.

It's hard to imagine a nebulous future when grandma passes. They have been looking after each other all her life. She doesn't know otherwise.

She knows for a fact that she will be without a home when that inevitably happens. However, there is also this deep sense of knowing and a belief that it's going to be okay, just like grandma always says.

The Danger of Introspection

Some of us look inward to find answers and healing because we think it will be more achievable to do it on our own, instead of counting on others or relying on external forces.

We have seen the ugliness of this world. When we search deep within, we realise we perhaps see the same ugliness. The only difference is, this time, we no longer can ignore the ugly by walking away. We carry that ugly inside and we don't know how to get rid of it.

We may hear that by searching our heart, we will find answers and even treasures. The reality is that *'out of the heart flows the issues of life'*. It's almost like the chicken or the egg scenario. We wonder if the heart corrupts the way we live our lives, or the other way around.

If we can change our heart without miracles, then there will be less misery of life. Miracles are hardly the things we can generate from within. Therefore, it is childish to think our heart can be renewed by introspection and we can find our own way out of suffering.

The danger of introspection is like bumping our head on a brick wall and wondering what is wrong with us that we are battered and bleeding. It may not be so obvious to most because that brick wall is so charming and appearing to be so full of life. And yet, we don't know why we are slowly going insane while life is draining out of us.

There is a time we come to know our limits and call out for help.

The Day Overcame the Night

I used to think I belonged to the hours of the owl. My safe place was by the nightstand where I showed myself freely in feline stretch. The bell rang from my wrist calling to my lover to overcome me while whispering every dark secret and indecent desire. Back then, smoky eyes and ripened cherry lips kept begging to drown out the safe word.

You carefully brought me out into the sunlight. My sun-kissed forehead, freckled cheeks, and salt-stained lips yearned for life in every breath I took. The bubble of the ocean wrapped me in total warmth and security. You held me in your arms and the sun held us in its palms.

Profile Pic

Not everything has to be sexual!

They aren't? So, tell me, what are your bare legs and overflowing breasts for?

They are my best features and assets. A bit of showing off is a reflection of my newfound confidence.

Oh! Apologies for overlooking the depth of its meaning. It's hard to be philosophical about it when you scream *'Fuck me!'*

(Silence is the answer.)

Master and Servant

She caught his sharp lion eyes with her subdued aura, permeating the buzzing party like cool air on a summer night. Her liquid scent weighed down his judgement. He became unsure of himself.

Powerful is her vulnerability, driving him to move mountains for her. The day will come. She will ask him for the impossible and he will gladly obey.

Country Train Trip

I enjoy taking the country train to the little lavender farm where the elderly couple sell lavender soaps and essential oils from their rusted shed.

When the country train chugs along the hills and bends, I am my happiest self, daydreaming with my forehead pressing the windowpane.

If life was always this simple, carrying us on a journey that we are content with, and to an idyllic destination to meet with humble beings. Indeed, I caught a glimpse of heaven on earth.

Table for Three

I try to look through the foggy glass windowpane to a faraway escape.

My agony drowns in the absence of tears and apologies.

Questions rushing through my fragile mind.

The endless waiting, the future without our past, the changed heart without warning, the intrusion of our love; all this heartache, I can't put into words.

None of us are willing to break the deafening silence.

It's a starry night and the moon hangs high.

The discordant sound of cutlery, extinguishes any romantic notion in the glorious sky.

Dinner for three is spread on pristine pressed linen. Food loses its charm and temptation all at once.

None of us speak any sense, watching dishes come and go.

I don't know how to end this torture, to disappear into the night.

It's a starry night and the moon is hung high.

The discordant sound of the cutlery extinguishes any romantic notion of the glorious sky.

Near-Miss Romance

Yesterday I took my son ice-skating. I did a few rounds in the ice rink with a perpetual worry of falling and breaking my bones. These types of worries only come with aging. Aging is also good for reminiscing.

Back then … I was a misfit trying to blend in with my peers. I wasn't alone, quite the opposite, I was somewhat popular with groups of friends throughout school years. I was lonely though when I was surrounded by people. I have always enjoyed my own company, definitely way too much when compared to what's considered a healthy amount of time to spend alone.

Growing up, I have never experienced princess, fairy tale, or wedding-bride dreams. I just wanted a buddy to hang out with, preferably a quiet dude on the geeky/nerdy side, wearing checkered shirts and glasses. So, when it comes to first dates, my skull has gone prickly and itchy thinking on the subject.

Regarding principles for first dates, most that I know about girls or read about girls, I observe that they usually have some restrictions on those first dates. For example, only a vanilla kiss is allowed; French kissing is off limits; an Aussie kiss* is absolutely a no-go; no sex on first dates; guys must pay, pick up and drop off; only showcasing the bright side in both appearance and character.

I did have some first date principles, sadly none of the above. Now I suspect maybe that is why my first dates never quite went well. My principles are quite straight forward in my view, and my view only of course.

I dressed as plain as I could on my first dates: casual with minimal-to-no makeup. I considered it a strategy. I could not stand the disappointment on his face when he saw my messy bed hair, rubbed off make-up, and runny mascara in the morning after a passionate night. So I figured if I was plain, then no complaints really. And I must say it did work.

I was poor at small talk; it made me want to carry a portable hole-in-the-ground with me. For that reason, my other principle for first dates is choice of venue. Aquarium, zoo, and amusement park are my top choices for their relaxed, fun, and semi-social elements. Art gallery, museum, and library are the second tier because they are the places I go to on my own a lot, so going with my date is still within my comfort zone. Unfortunately, none of these choices made it to my first date's venue list.

When I was seventeen, I went on one of my first dates. We went to a cinema and selected a random movie which is okay because I like spontaneity. I like watching movies, so it started off grand. He got us soft drinks (I didn't like drinking soft drinks) and nuts (with shells). Maybe he was both nervous and trying to be attentive. He drank his soft drink quickly and slurped the last bit LOUD and kept passing me nuts and crunching on them himself LOUD. I was nervous and trying to focus on the movie. But the scrunching, slurping, and plastic bumping noises made me barely able to keep myself still in the seat.

I closed my eyes focusing on my breathing and trying to think of the positive things. Things like: he was not trying to have a conversation in the middle of the movie and he did all the right things like picking me up and walking between me and the traffic. Halfway through the movie, he quietly put his arm around my shoulder and leaned a little bit closer to me. While I was trying to make myself get comfortable with the fond gesture, the characters on the screen started to undress and make out. Oh, how I wished I *did* have a portable hole in the ground! I half stood and retreated from the seat quietly and walked out of the cinema with my cheeks burning and heart racing in massive embarrassment.

At nineteen, I went on another of my first dates. I agreed to his invitation of an ice-skating rink. I had warmed to the idea because I had noticed him for a long time, and it took him quite a while to ask me out. I also imagined ice skating as a pair would be romantic and cute and if I fell, I could hope he would catch me, just like in the movies. I could ice skate basically, meaning going forward without aids and slowly turning around. I was in my comfortable jeans and jumper with a plain face and that put me at complete ease.

We set off to the rink and glided along the curves, following the circle. Oh, one thing I need to mention: he was super good-looking with an athletic build. The possibility of him not knowing how to ice skate was totally inconceivable. Yet despite this, he soon fell hard on the ice, and I didn't try to hold him to stop him falling. I assessed the situation and judged that I wasn't going to be strong enough to save him falling. So, I just let him fall. In hindsight, I probably should have held him, so at least both of us would have fallen together and fulfilled the romantic movie scene with giggling and maybe even kissing in the end.

Not only did I let him fall, but I also kept gliding further away from him not knowing how to brake. The worst part was coming... An athletic, gorgeous-looking girl with a short skirt skated to his rescue. Who would wear a short skirt to an ice-skating rink? My eyes rolled around in a full circle while I was still attempting to stop myself hurtling forward. The date ended with the three of us sitting in the first-aid room. Actually, it was me in the corner and them drinking milkshakes next to each other. Damn my lactose intolerance! Grrrrrr....

At age 24, you would think I should have dated enough to avoid the awkward first date moment. But no, I have never learned. I said yes to this guy who I met in a local bar. We had been talking for quite a while over beers. I was trying to talk him out of asking me out. I even lied to him and said that I was an international student working in the local charcoal chicken shop. He would not budge. He persuaded me to have dinner with him at the pizzeria and take a walk down the beach afterward. I ultimately said yes just to get rid of him. I didn't give him my number and told him we would meet here at the bar before dinner. I was so going to ditch him.

When the night came, I didn't have the heart to do a no-show on him. Both of us arrived at almost the same time. When we saw each other, he sighed and grinned with relief. Hunger struck, so ordering pizzas and polishing them off left us only about twenty minutes for small talk. I learned he surfed and was studying for an art degree but mostly hung out with mates and baked way too many cookies. He told me he had stuttered when he was little and with speech therapy, he'd improved. I told him I was working three jobs and studying at TAFE* evening classes. The conversation was light-hearted and easy. I thought to myself that it was going well. With full pizza bellies, a walk down the beach seemed to be a perfect idea. To help with my nervousness, I slipped my hands in the pockets of my shorts as I strolled along the wet sand by his side.

The sound of the waves was lovely and soothing. There was silence between us. I quite enjoyed it and tried to take in the moment of romance. To break off the silence, he started to whistle *Yellow* by Cold Play. It's one of my favourites. I was thinking: will he kiss me? *'Do ya wanna swim?'* His question took me out of my dreamland. It took a moment for my brain to recognise what it was he was asking. He saw the dazed look on my face and mistook it for an affirmative nonverbal response. The next thing I realised was he was carrying me into the water with both my hands still in the pockets of my shorts. I was hopelessly off balance with all of me pressed into his arms and chest.

He started to run towards the waves. *Fuckkkkkk!!!* Fear rushed into my mind. A massive wave covered us and split us apart. I couldn't get my hands out of my soaked shorts' pockets. I swallowed a mouthful of bitter gritty foamy saline. When the wave finally tossed and spit me out to the shore, I was crawling in an attempt just to stand straight. *Fuckkkkkk!!!* I was both shocked and furious. I couldn't see him on the shore or coming out of the water. I was swearing *'Fuck! Fuck! Fuck! Fucking fuck!!!'* I breathed deeply and straightened my shorts, singlets, and hair, finally composing myself as he emerged from the water, walking towards me.

'I lost you' he said. I replied testily, *'Yeah, it's a massive wave. Let's go! I didn't bring dry clothes, don't wanna catch a cold.'* I was trying to be reasonable and end the night on a decent note. *'Come to my pad and I'll dry you off,'* he said casually. *'It's alright; I got an early shift tomorrow. I'd better head home now,'* I replied. By then, I had the cold shivers quite badly. We walked silently to my car. I put my hand in my pocket for the car key while he was pulling me to him. I looked up to meet his eyes while the realisation hit me that my car key was missing. His mouth was almost on mine, *'Fuck! Fuck you!'* escaped my lips. There was no turning back. I might just let it out. *'Why the fuck did you throw me in the water? Now I lost my fucking car key in the fucking sea. Fuck me!'*

These are my awkward first date memories with near-miss romance fantasy. It would never turn out that awkwardly if we had gone to the aquarium, zoo, or the amusement park, now would it?

* *Aussie Kiss = a kiss that takes place 'down under'*

* *TAFE = Technical and Further Education*

Hiking in Spring

He told her he was going hiking to catch a glimpse of the September blooms. She knew the route like the back of her hand. Many times, they hiked to the vantage point where the Tatarian maple stood, giving shade for resting and ground for play.

She remembered how he laughed at her impractical hiking dress code: sports cap, sundress, and hiking boots. In her mischievous mind, she knew that was the perfect outfit. It was proven by all the passionate moments under that tree.

She couldn't go hiking with him anymore for he was no longer her man, physically, anyway. But both knew, they always went hiking together. The moment he took a rest under the Tatarian maple, she was there just like many times before. It was hard to focus on the fresh spring flowers when his nostrils were filled with her slightly moist scent from perspiring.

She was having a cup of earl grey on the daybed under the warm sun, taking a break from reading. Her mind wandered back to him. She sensed that he was sitting with his back against the trunk of that maple, drinking mineral water. She could see the movement of his Adam's apple. That's usually the time she would agilely climb on his lap, lifting, then scattering her sundress for cover. He would never refuse her, always giving her every ounce of himself in exchange of watching the satisfaction on her face while she paraded over him like a peacock.

Sometimes, they wished their connection was broken when they parted ways. And sometimes, they secretly, earnestly gravitated towards each other, especially in spring, a season where everything grows.

My Father Has Dementia at 61

There was always safety in our father's presence. The memory of him rafting with me and my younger brother out on the Balmoral water in early autumn is still vivid in my mind today, the same as the cold winter day we buried our mother.

We have never felt neglected by our widowed father. And he has never made us feel any guilt, although we ran around like mad monkeys in our family home where our mother spent her last weeks.

Now I am sitting by his bed as a grown woman with my own family, listening to him telling incoherent stories of the past. Maybe to him, this is the way he is coping with the opened floodgate of emotions, which have been bottled up for so long.

Betrayal

You had told me *'I love you'* for one thousand days. I really thought it meant something weighty and lasting.

The bouquets, the words, the hard-working late nights were your acts of service. I had mistaken them for something else.

How dare you ask me to forgive and forget all your lies.

That night, I tore my robe in anger, while you tore my heart apart.

No Filter

She walked up to a man on a crowded platform, *"Your zipper is undone,"* then kept walking.

She sat across the romantic dinner table to her Plenty of Fish date, *"You have spinach between your top middle teeth."* She ate another fork full of gnocchi.

She was on a call with her sobbing girlfriend who had broken up with her boyfriend. *"You've been talking about a history like a current event, it is time to put it in the right period,"* she said ten minutes into the call.

She is a girl with little filter. She figures it's better that way.

Memory

We bade each other farewell at graduation in 1988.

Our grown-up duty called us from the popular college band we played in.

Goodbye to those nights when we smoked some weed and waxed some new tracks.

Coffee and cigarettes stained not only our teeth, but also our memory.

What remained was this faded photo with all of us lined up in our flamboyant bell bottom jeans.

I took off my fogged-up reading glasses, wiped off my tears and slowly sipped my herbal tea.

Outing

I caught the happy train today.

The world outside the window was a kaleidoscope. I couldn't help but clap and flap my hands at the ever-changing beauty before my hungry eyes.

I am dreading the return to my padded cell.

I can never understand why they call it a calm room. Why is sanity built on the foundation of deceit?

A Field of Cherry Sunflowers

Wherever I saw sunflowers in the day, I thought of you.

You stood facing the sun in full bloom of a smile disregarding the harsh light.

The night was a thief who came to steal, rob, and abuse.

When the night went on, beyond what you could bear, you let him slit your wrists.

Your passion for life was drained out in crimson rain.

Whenever you came into my dreams at night, I saw you wandering in a field of cherry sunflowers in an anaemic gown.

Hunch

He barely kept eye contact and rarely spoke to me when he hung out with us.

We hung out a lot and he was always there, wearing his nerdy glasses and checked shirt.

I found nerds attractive and terribly sexy in checked shirts.

I thought he was hopelessly shy and sensitive like a bunny rabbit.

Call it a hunch; I knew he was in love with me.

That's what I've prepared for our wedding speech.

Zany

In 1982, there were no sculpted nudes in China, not even under Deng Xiaoping's economic reform of opening China to the outside world.

He, the Beethoven-looking man, created stacks of nude sculptures in his studio, which was no more than a kiosk tucked away in the alley.

We walked past his studio after school and made fun of him wearing silk stockings and hairnets, by pulling faces and giggling as we ran away.

Now in 2020, I am a lot more educated on celebrating individuality and have seen the world outside of red China.

We were little assholes of ignorant parents and grandparents.

I have forgiven myself and am proud of how far I have come from that six-year-old girl.

Mama

Mama, I finally moved back home from the theatre limelight. I don't know what took me so long to resign from the stale cigarettes and rancid wine. I guess I wasn't thinking all that straight.

Before I decided to move back, I dreamed of you one night. We rode our bikes to that big pine tree by the beach. I wore the turquoise fairy dress you bought me for my 5th birthday. It was a breezy sunny day. I smelled the ocean scented fragrance from your fingertips when you reached to fix my hat. I looked up, the blue sky piercing through your windblown hair in strips. You smiled at me like a sunflower, and I knew you were pleased with me. Mama, it has been so long since I dreamed of you again. When I woke up, I still felt the warmth of your hand on my freckled cheeks, and heard you saying *"Darling, look at your beautiful glow! Your smile makes the sun shy."*

Mama, most of the time I was so alone. The stage was filled with a clapping audience. I was too scared to look, as I knew you weren't there, no matter how much I may have searched for your face. My success was meaningless without you. People thought I was busy achieving to please you. But only I knew, I was just avoiding seeing you ill. I didn't know how to be your daughter, the grown up and responsible one. I was still a little girl in that fairy dress who needed her mommy to fix her hat.

Now I am home, strolling the same beach we once walked every day. I see the same waves slapping the rocks in anger, the same sun pouring abundantly at the ocean, the same pine tree carrying more shade. But you are my missing piece. I am that little girl who fell off the bike and tripped over the tree roots and whose food got snatched by seagulls. Mama, why do I have to grow up?

Passionate Death

It is times like this I wonder if the line is too blurry or my mind is filled with opiate, in between trembling and dead calm, losing control and yet, holding with such a firm grip.

Tell me, where do you want to land? Will you let go?

Land in a complete state that any more is too much. The waves become dead calm in a pool of serenity.

I feel your heart open, red, beating, bared for me to see. Tell me, what do you hold back?

There is always a veil between us, except when your fire penetrates through and burns before it has time to form again.

Sometimes I swim in your deep pools. I feel the warm currents.

I effortlessly brush over your feet like a summer breeze.

From your feet to my face, I land with a kiss.

My breath has found a way to climb into your firm form. It agilely tests its territory without disturbing, while sensing your tensing and flexing.

Be careful, I am delicate but strong, not to be played with.

Then we are bare, heart to heart, in our coffin bed. In the confinement of death ahead, there is no more to lose than ourselves. At what point will you let me go? As we spin together into galaxies of nothing and light.

You are always free my love! You are free from my lingering fingers tapping poetry with your heartstrings.

I am not free. I can't let go. You are everything I always wanted. I forsook my life to get lost in this whirlpool... this black hole...

Play me the song, the funeral song, as I spend my final moments with you. Completing our love. One final dance. One final journey into the mysterious.

Oh, how I lament over this forbidden encounter in the early mornings and let torturous thoughts drown me in denial.

I study your body, your beautiful feminine outline, so swelling and yet sharp, surrounded by tiny goose bumps. And your skin so smooth, two mounds that dip down, every muscle quivering. How my tongue explores...

When the veil slips, my being has a way to meet your every desire in obedience and passive eruption.

Lead me, tangle me in your web, bewitch me with your desolate desperation for conquering.

Then, I will conquer you. I will pull down your last covering. I will slip in to places unknown. I have many ways to satisfy.

I'll plough your dew-soaked lake, deep and forceful while I lay my hand beneath your head, dance my lips to yours like sweet poetry. Lilies in the valley fill my intake of breath. I become lightheaded, intoxicated, and lost in you.

My hands interlock above my head in surrender. My every expression fuels your vigour to total abandon.

Scream for me! Tell me how you want it.

My aura intensifies before your staring hunger. Every fan of fire calls you to dwell deeper. Take me, take my life! Take me to

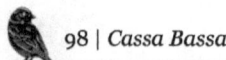

places beyond death's reach.

Nothing felt like this before. Tell me; are you ready to join in our dying climax?

Always ready for the eruption, paving the way for orgasmic combustion.

Crimson fire fills my view. I am lost in the moment. I give away and let myself go fully in you. This is our final act.

My moans turn primal, and my scream has no name...

My Life in Olfaction

My childhood school holidays were mostly spent on my maternal grandparent's farm. My grandfather and uncles were farmers. They smoked home-grown tobacco from handmade bamboo water pines. I loved the sweet burning aroma of fresh tobacco on rainy spring days. Children often sat on the door's threshold and listened to the elders' conversation while eating seasonal fruits. Summer was hot and humid. Farmers laid out fresh cow manure in the front of the house to dry it, then used it for household burning fuel. We children got into trouble for throwing cow manure at each other, playing war games. The simple laidback and carefree farm life set the tone for my adult life.

When school holidays finished, I returned to overpopulated city living. Our nano flat was filled with a mixed odour of beehive briquettes, exhaust, stale cigarettes and cooking grease. I visited my grandparent's townhouse on weekends. It had a completely different smell. The lounge room smelled of grandpa's Hongmei cigarettes and roasted peanuts. In the courtyard, the kitchen was infused with Cantonese cooking spices – ginger, garlic, and coriander. If I was lucky, great grandma would cook her signature dish: steamed pork and grapefruit peel stir fry in dark soy. Its fragrance accompanying the boiled jasmine rice formed a cloud hovering in the kitchen that induced my belly to rumble with anticipation. The love for cooking ran in my father's family. We learned cooking while helping in the kitchen from a young age. Family meals brought four generations together.

School years smelled of paper pulp and ink print. Faded yellow books with jet black characters, it smelled of wisdom and brighter futures. I received floral-scented letters from a not-so-secret admirer. He often included a pencil sketch of my backside with my ponytail up high. But most passing notes between

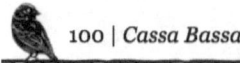

classmates had no smell unless it was handed to you by an after lunch greasy hand, which smelled like peanut oil deep fried tofu. School years gave me the resilience to cope with changes in friendship, authority, and routine and to overcome disappointment and failure.

Love smelled like drugs and blood from broken skin. I crawled back to the same destructive hurt over and over again like a lamb willingly feeding itself to the slaughter. Although the scream remained silent, the brokenness was visible. There were momentary scents of flower bouquets and intoxicating pleasure. The invariable crashing end was a vomit of putrid regret. Love made me blind and vulnerable. However, I would still give it all and love again.

Work always smelled like strong coffee and fast burning cigarettes. It was probably more for social acceptance than the hope of promotion because it affected productivity. Consequently, there was a constant compromise of quantity and quality. So, I adopted ways to get to an acceptable standard with least time spent. Over my working life, I was blessed with a variety of careers where I got to be with people from all walks of life. It reminded me of tasting pizzas in an authentic Italian family-owned restaurant.

My baby smelled like blossom and life itself. Measuring his little feet in my palms was my favourite moment of all time. Lifting his chubby feet to my nose, I inhaled deeply, and images of bright moments flooded my mind, from new shoots on bare tree branches, freshly hatched chicks, to blowing bubbles on a bright sunny day. He brought wholeness and joy to me. I grew into a selfless and forgiving person from motherhood.

Marriage smelled like fresh citrus at the beginning and turned into a bottle of sour wine at the end of the journey. We drank the potion when it was fresh and new, too impatient to wait for it to age properly and become an extraordinary taste. It could have been ageless if we preserved it well at each stage of development. We took for granted what we had and left it carelessly to be malnourished. When patience ran its course, I no longer could swallow its bitter bile, and I walked out, deflated with a mouthful of tasteless disappointment. No matter how I tried to savour the crisp beginnings, my taste buds were numb and coated in tar.

A new beginning smells like ocean mist and freshly cut grass. It is both rejuvenating and invigorating. The image of a new home is like farm life, where unvarnished timber furniture gives out a scent of nature; burning fireplaces; spices infusing home cooking; lilac, lavender, sage, and sandalwood permeate the sleeping chambers. It takes me back to the wonderful childhood memories of a close-knit family, with children running around the farmhouse.

After Fifteen Years

She picked a table at the far corner of the café. From there she had a full view of the entrance while still being able to hide herself away under the dim light. She sat slightly hunched over the small square wooden table, one hand trapped between her knees, the other restlessly tapping the table with her bare fingers. They hurt a little from nail biting, and the pain actually helped her to ease her panic and anxiety.

The waiter approached with a warm smile. *"What would you like today, Mia? Long black or chai?"*

"Long black. Thanks, Joe. Uhm… maybe not now. I am still waiting for someone, a bit rude to order first, I suppose?"

"No worries, I'll come back when you are ready." He winked, giving his usual million-dollar grin. However, for once she didn't watch him as he moved off.

"Aiyaya, sorry, sir. I didn't see you there. My apologies."

She followed Joe's voice and saw him. Pins and needles piled up in the top of her skull. Blood rushing to her brain. She had to hold on to the edge of the table with both hands to steady herself.

"Mia, sorry I am a bit late; I was stuck in a meeting and I left my phone somewhere." He reached for a kiss but then realised she was still sitting down. He sat opposite her. His hand slid towards hers, but she didn't stop gripping the corner of the table. She looked up and their eyes met. His were aqua blue when he was happy, slate when he was in deep thought. Now they were almost hazel under the warm café lighting.

He smiled, showing his front teeth; there was a gap between the middle two. She used to think it lightened up his serious demeanour. *"Mia, are you there?"* he teased.

"Hey, you! I'm…I am glad you agreed to meet. Look at you! You haven't changed a bit." She relaxed a little into her chair having finally greeted him. Her fingers tried to tug her loose curls behind her ears.

"Would you like a mocha? They make it just right here."

"As long as you are having a long black to keep me company."

"Sure. I will call Joe over." She was about to get up.

He grabbed both her hands and held them up to his nose. He smelled the ginger and cinnamon on her bare fingers and started to laugh uncontrollably. He used to call her badly bitten nails the circumcised fingers. When she flavoured the meat in curry cooking, she would swear her head off because the stinging sensation on her broken skin was unbearable. And yet, being Mia, she would not wear gloves.

She knew exactly what he was laughing about but couldn't pull away from his firm grip. She bellowed a laugh instead.

Widow

She walks straight into the industrial loft showroom, searching for the rustic vintage teak study desk. The dark shaded timber furniture on display, blended in with red and burgundy floor rugs. They floated on the dark metallic painted floor. It made her feel claustrophobic and reminded her of the room where the wake was held at the funeral. Halfway into the showroom, she spots her desk standing next to a red Victorian Tiffany-style floor lamp.

She races towards it ignoring the other shoppers and the enticing aroma from the coffee cart two metres to her right. The long drape of her skirt brushes the heels of her bare feet. She leans on the short edge of the desk, closes her eyes, and breathes in slowly, then out. She tries to block the chattering customers, the professional tone of the friendly salespeople and the whining of a coffee grinder. She lays her slender tanned hands on the rough surface of the rustic teak. Her half-moon shaped fingers are tracing the grains in delicate circles. She smells the sandalwood and incense and hears the trickles of the Feng Shui water fountain. Then the void hits her and brings an unrecoverable lump to her throat.

Mid-Autumn Festival

Mid-Autumn Festival is a harvest festival celebrated notably by the Chinese and other Asian peoples. It falls on the fifteenth day of the eighth lunar month each year. It is the second biggest traditional Chinese festival beside the Spring Festival (Chinese New Year).

Growing up, the Mid-Autumn Festival was my favourite celebration. As kids, we made lanterns, lit them, and roamed the streets with them. We also played with a few smaller firecrackers and fireworks, which is no longer allowed due to fire safety restrictions.

There were always fresh seasonal fruits including starfruit, grapefruit, longans, watermelons, and bananas. Fresh taros boiled in salt water made my mouth water. Mooncakes are the indispensable delicacy which are generally made using lotus seed paste, red bean paste, or nut mix that fills the crust.

Family members would sit outdoors with the spread of fruits, taros, mooncakes, and teas to appreciate the full moon while chatting away about everything or nothing. Children were usually allowed to stay up until midnight as an exception.

Mid-Autumn Festival is a time for family reunion, sharing special food, and celebrating good times. I loved those times as I was brought up in a four-generation big family in a close-knit community. I got to hang out with kids on the street and listen to adults sharing stories from home and afar.

Last night I looked at the moon in a land that is foreign and distant to those memories. I still smiled and those memories were like yesterday, despite being decades ago.

A Love Story

I had a dream about a love story.

The scene was set in the sunlit hillside overlooking green pastures, a boy, and a girl under an oak tree. She was sitting against the giant oak tree, and he was lying, head on her lap. He was looking at her with his honey brown eyes full of admiration and love. She launched her gaze far, far away to the green hills while combing her fingers through his golden curls. They were just talking softly.

This was after they made love throughout the night with unquenchable thirst and fire. She was in awe of how pure and innocent he was. He drank in her mesmerising beauty and gravitated to her inner strength.

There under the oak tree, he expressed his unfailing love for her with his passion and commitment. And yet, she was torn between her uncontrollable longing for his pureness and innocence, and the dimmest remaining logic.

I would write on and on about how this sweet love developed and she came to her senses and believed that he loved her unconditionally...

But that's not what happened....

The reality goes like this:

It was a warm autumn day on the east coast of Australia.

An American writer had been spending a long overdue holiday in the land down under. His recent book launch was a success which had funded this holiday. He always wanted to live in this land for its rich aboriginal culture and diverse landscapes. He suffers spells of blues for most of his life. Wearing the sunshine and ocean breeze seemed to be helping to relieve the itchy jumper prickles.

He hadn't felt this relaxed and free from torment of the past for a long time. He was almost feeling a tinge of lightness in the foreign land of his dreams. He felt he could breathe again, and he was able to think past today to what breakfast he would like tomorrow morning.

Being a bald bearded guy with tattoos, he blended in nicely with local Aussies except when he ordered his meals in a North American accent. She instantly looked up when she heard that familiar accent and she gave him a grin. He is the type of guy who will avoid eye contact at all costs, not because of shyness but due to the intensity he feels when souls collide.

She is an Australian-born Armenian, recently returned from Tehran. She spent her school years and most of her adult life in Tehran. She learned to speak English mostly from the soap operas she watched when growing up, hence the familiarity of the American accent. All her Aussie friends asked her *'How was life in the States?'* when they first met her. She left her 22 years of life in Tehran behind with no regrets. The physical violence and mental anguish she escaped from, gave her permanent scars. Although she did regain her will and power to live on in her homeland. Beautiful sunshine, the warmth of the locals, and the uncomplicated laidback lifestyle were assurance for her continued recovery and healing.

They hit it off immediately from the American accent and the shared benefit of the sun and ocean to long walks to watch the sunset. There was no doubt that the attraction was instant, regardless of the constraint felt by both. Love was certainly dancing in the salty air, energising, rejuvenating, and invigorating, to the souls, the minds, and their mortal bodies.

Life takes unexpected turns. Love comes in mysterious ways. He felt he had just started to leave the bag of bones behind, while she just started to settle into the freedom she long missed. They applied their logic, and both knew love had come at such an inconvenient time.

They travelled together to Uluru (Ayers Rock) to walk the same path, the traditional landowners of Australia, the Aboriginal people first set foot on, over 20000 years ago. They read about the Aboriginal Australian way of living, especially the waiting. They wait in line with patience, waiting for rain to fill the rivers, waiting for the bush to open to harvest, waiting for the young people to grow up and flourish. They let nature guide them, never in a hurry. They listen deeply to connect with the inner springs inside them.

They were at the crossroad of their lives. The choices he made against his heart and the bitter past, led to a fear-filled, tormented living death. She was a wounded soul trampled and deprived by the one she vowed her life to. They shared the common longing for healing and restoration.

Finally, when they were both standing in front of Uluru, all the questions, uncertainty, insecurity, and inabilities, started peeling away. Their moment of waiting and listening deeply to connect with their inner springs, surfaced and became a connection and bond between them. The rain drizzled down on the land into the dry rivers, and the rivers overflowed into one, the season of harvest, the future of flourishing.

When hope is lost, this is where hope is found. When love is intangible, this is where love becomes a reality.

D-Day

I opened my eyes to the fiery amber morning glow. First sunrise of winter. The crisp air reminded me of *The day*.

That year there were unusual rainfalls. We spent a day in the mountains. We rose early for a walk in the powdery rain, starting the fire by the last sip of coffee. You came to the rug where I sat, knelt and then plaited my hair. I curled up like a cat on the rug with my shoes half done up. In silence you tied my shoelaces.

We held hands and walked in the rain deep into the bush in silence. When we came back, we were both sweating with chills.

I made us coffee and we sat back-to-back by the fire on the fluffy rug. You read to me, everything from the local news to poetry. Your voice and the crackling of the fire became the most memorable sounds.

The rain got heavier, and we could hear the dancing rhythm on the roof. Both of us love the sound of the rain. And we met on a rainy day. I knew when we heard the rain, we both thought of the first time we laid eyes on each other. We turned around with our eyes meeting. My heart pounding out of my jumper and your lips landing on mine. The last sentence I heard that day was your whisper in my ear: *'I want you. '*

That day is the most glorious day of my life. I experienced the five most romantic acts in that rainy Winter Day. You plaited my hair, tied my shoelaces, walked in the rain with me, read to me by the fire and said, *'I want you.'* I savoured every moment and every detail.

You can only contain that much happiness in one day, one life

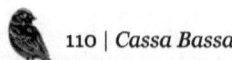

with one love. For that, we both knew that day was *The day*. The day we wandered off from each other knowingly, or subconsciously.

We did it in silence. No formal conversation, no tears, no embracing, no goodbyes. We walked away in the middle of climax, in triumph, in perfection. We both knew there was never going to be another We or Us. We preserved our love and upheld its prestige.

"True love may only come once in a lifetime. But it can come once and once is more than enough." – Fawn Weaver

We Are One

I watched the news and saw how they keep the activists in the kettle during a protest.

It reminds me of fencing society outcasts in a so called self-contained farm.

There is little difference from quarantine.

They are supplied with minimal essential items and expected to survive in a self-sufficient way whilst prisoners, which we all know to be impossible.

They are out of sight, out of mind, while the rest of us wonder why sometimes we have broken sleep and experience an unexplainable sense of dread.

We are all connected as inhabitants on mother earth, where we share each other's joy or suffering.

<u>Closure</u>

I sit in the same chair with both hands tucked underneath my thighs. This is the last of the ten free sessions I am eligible for during this calendar year. I don't anticipate hearing anything new from Dr. Weber. She is going to give me a non-progressing Progress Report. Well, to be more accurate, it will be a regressing Progress Report.

I am acutely aware that my Achromatopsia is getting worse. In no time I will only see black, white, and grey. I am a rare case. The ophthalmologist could not diagnose me as Achromatopsia positive, because I was not born with this condition. During the last two years, I have been gradually losing my ability to see colour. On my medical report, my condition was referred to 'Undetermined Achromatopsia,' and I was referred to Dr. Weber, a clinical psychologist for further assessment.

Dr. Weber conducted a DSM-IVR assessment and she did not give me any mental illness diagnosis. She recommended that I receive psychological counselling to help improve my ability to cope with losing my colour vision. I have been seeing Dr. Weber for more than 2 years. Personally, I don't think it is helping with my Achromatopsia. I keep attending the psychological counselling sessions as I get ten free sessions annually which are fully funded by public health Medicare, and I enjoy talking to Dr Weber. Every time after I see her, I feel okay with losing my colour vision. I am grateful that I did not have Achromatopsia from birth. I know the full spectrum of colours. I remember the rainbow and the distinctive colours of the four seasons.

It is in the middle of autumn now. When I look at the fallen leaves, I see a cluster of yellow-orange-red. They are less vibrant than what I am used to. But they are still pretty. It is more like watercolour, impressionist painting. It gives a mesmerising illusionary feel.

"Sage, thank you for waiting. I apologise for the wait. Please come in and make yourself comfortable." Dr. Weber is wearing an A-line dress with a scarf hung on her shoulder. The print looks like Japanese maple trees, which I find fitting for the season. I always admire her sense of style, elegant and calming.

"It's okay. I was just daydreaming anyway." I sink myself in the apple green beanbag with my legs stretching to a V shape. I feel comfortable and in a relaxed mood.

"This is the last session we have this calendar year. I will do a year review with you. First though, tell me about your life since I saw you five weeks ago." Dr. Weber sits facing me, sideways to her cream fabric oversized lounge chair situated next to the three-seater matching couch.

"Uhm…I had a good month I suppose. Nothing is sticking out in particular at work, home, or dating, ha-ha, the absence of dating, I should clarify," I share with her in a cheeky way.

"You look relaxed and carry a sense of fun, it seems." She smiles showing her pearly white teeth, with a visible gap between the two middle top teeth. I think that makes her cute, although she is in her 50s.

"What about your colour vision?" she carries on.

"I still can see colours. They are just blurrier and meshing together. It's like looking at impressionist paintings. I don't mind really. It kinda makes me more arty." I give her a big grin.

"At the last session, you shared with me that you saw colours, but they were mixing with grey and black. Is that still the case in the last weeks?" Dr. Weber asks while referring to the notes on her tablet.

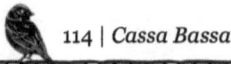

"Yeah last month was rough with project deadlines to meet at work, and I hadn't gotten laid for ages. So, I was as grumpy as shit. It might be lack of sleep which worsens my colour vision. I don't know really. The grey and black seemed to disappear after the Easter break. To be honest, I feel after a good night sleep, my colour vision has better focus. I can tell the colours distinctively."

"What do you mean by telling the colours distinctively?" she probes.

"I mean I can tell the clear borders of colours. They are not like what I am seeing now with blurry outlines. I could tell when the blue sky finishes on the horizon. But now, it looks like the blue bleeds into the gold sunset. I don't know how to describe it better." I run my fingers from the top of my scalp to the back of my neck. When my hair ends just before my neck, it reminds me that I had my shoulder length hair chopped off to a slick back cut.

"Now I understand, Sage. Would you like to tell me more about the day before Jason's disappearance, just after his solo painting exhibition opening? I believe this has crucial correlation with your colour vision impairment." Dr. Weber moves her tablet to her lap. This usually means she is ready to tap on her tablet for some drop down box options or multiple choices selection. I know that because I work in the graphic design industry. I can tell by the way she taps her tablet.

"I don't know what else I can tell you, Dr. Weber. That day is like a grey cloud to me still today. One minute Jason was there with me sharing a joint to wind down from the exhibit opening night. It was an instant success. He sold five pieces of original work and a bunch of print copies on an anticipation of none. Then he told me he needed to duck out to the bottle shop for more grog. The next minute he was gone just like the fame of his painting. I waited and waited and waited. I thought he met up with friends, got pissed, and stayed out for the night. He didn't answer his mobile when I called nor responded to my *messages on Messenger, WhatsApp, or Instagram. I was so mad at him that I popped some Valium and was knocked out. I hate myself for it. I really do. I didn't even think of the possibility that he was in danger. I just assumed he was being an ass. Now he is gone. I hope he is still just being an ass rather than being murdered by some sicko."* I finish talking and I find myself pacing the room instead of sitting on the beanbag.

"Sage, what do you think you would have done if you had gone out to look for Jason after realising he was not answering his phone?"

"I could have gone to the bottle shop and asked the owner where he headed after he bought the grog. But I don't think that would have amounted to anything." I am still pacing with my head down, looking at my boots.

"What else could you have done if you were not asleep?" Dr. Weber's voice is levelled and assertive.

"I don't think the police would have done anything about it if I reported a missing person. I would have sounded like a drug-affected lunatic."

"Anything else you can think of that you could possibly have done?"

"I could have messaged his mates via Apps and I would probably find out he was not with them. But how could I? I would have been seen like a clinging fuck buddy. Oh God! I wish I had been that clinging bitch." My hands are on each side of my head with fingers digging into my scalp, still pacing.

"Sage, let me get you a glass of chilled water or a coke. We can take a break, if you'd like." I can hear Dr. Weber moving towards the mini bar fridge in the far corner of the room.

"A mini coke please, Dr. Weber." I stop pacing and lie down on the 3-seater couch. I feel a migraine is coming on. I lift one arm to

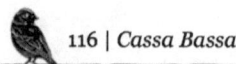

block out the light.

The light is dimmed to a night light setting. I take the coke can Dr. Weber hands to me and roll it across my forehead. The icy cold feeling on my skin supresses the migraine.

"Let's keep going Dr. Weber. I don't want to be a quitter like all the other times. I know this is hitting a spot. I don't want to let the migraine be an excuse. I know I need to press on."

"Let's do it, Sage!" Dr. Weber sits back down at her lounge chair. *"It seems to me that there was little difference you could make to prevent Jason's disappearance. I understand it to be a tragedy especially when there is no closure for you or the other people who loved and cared for him."*

"I know. It is only wishful thinking that I could save him. I loved him although we were never officially dating. I knew him all my life. He was so goofy from day one in kindergarten, the only rosy-cheeked chubby Asian kid in the whole school. My Mum still looks over our photos in yearbooks. He was like the son my parents couldn't have. To me, his disappearance took a chunk of me with him. I feel he took my keen eye for colours with him, like the most brilliant part of me. Now I am losing the ability to see colours. I feel the certainty of him dying in some dungeon." My head is throbbing, and my scalp is feeling tender. I open the coke and take a couple sips.

"Tell me more about the certainty you feel relating to your belief Jason is dying, how did you come to that sense or conclusion?"

"I feel the gift I have for colour is always what Jason saw in me that attracted him. It is like a bond we have. He always said his passion for art in painting was inspired by me from our young age. We used to spend hours colouring, drawing, and describing everything we saw in colour-related words. When we hit secondary school, we started to describe our feelings in colours. That's what Jason's paintings are

about, an expression of moods, emotions, and feelings through colour construction. I did it as a fun game. To him though, colour was like a world he lived in and breathed in. I feel haunted sometimes as if Jason possesses me even though he is not with me. I almost feel he is controlling my colour vision at times. I know I sound crazy. You told me I am not clinically insane. I can talk to you about these thoughts and feelings. But I will never share with others. There is no way they would think I am normal. I shared with my Mum once and she thought I took some psychedelic drugs and tripped out."

"Have you taken psychedelic drugs, Sage?" Dr. Weber asks.

"Nope. I only smoke dope when I am stressed or need to wind down. I don't drink either, if you remember in our initial assessment."

"I do remember. It was over two years ago. I want to be sure of my understanding of your condition. It wasn't meant to come across as an offense."

"I wasn't offended, just to clarify, that's all."

"Sage, grief may cause us to experience all kinds of difficult and unexpected emotions, including the feeling of not be able to think straight. Grieving is a highly individual experience; there's no right or wrong way to grieve, and no 'normal' timetable for grieving. Jason was and is, a big part of your life in a friendship and intimate relationship sense. I commend you for seeking counselling to try to make sense of your condition and reality. I hope you find our sessions helpful and you get something out of it."

"I do, Dr. Weber. I feel I have an outlet to express myself. It's not like I will go around showing my sad face every day to the people around me. I am trying to move on and get better. I am thankful I can still see colours sometimes. To be honest, if I completely lost my ability to see colours, I am okay with it. In some way I know an important part of me, is with him."

"It seems to me you are at peace with it, is that the case, Sage?"

"I wouldn't say I am at peace with not seeing colours anymore. I used to love this colourful world, anything that is visually stimulating. Now, I suppose, it is okay to see the world in a monochromatic way. C'est la Vie."

"So, would you say you come to an acceptance of your condition and this new reality?" Dr. Weber is looking straight into my eyes when she asks the question.

"I think I do. No! I know I do. I accept the world is a lack of colours, even monochromatic since Jason has gone, and I am okay with it." My eyes meet hers and my cheeks relax to a smile.

I walk out of Dr. Weber's office. The autumn chill air greets me. I wrap my scarf around my neck and look up, the elm tree sways in the late afternoon sun, shimmering its leaves like golden tassels. I imagine them to be burnt orange by now. Autumn is our favourite season for the pure joy of the autumn colour palette. I pick up a fallen leaf and blow it to the sky, whispering *"Jason, this is for you. Tell me what colour it is in my dreams tonight."*

More Published Works by Cassa Bassa

Contribute author of Australian Poetry Journal Volume 8, 2020

Contribute author of *The Poets Symphony* published by Raw Earth Ink, 2020

Contribute author of *Creation and the Cosmos* published by Raw Earth Ink, 2021

Contribute author of *Heart Beats* by Prolific Pulse Press, 2021

Contribute author of *Social Justice Inks* published by Prolific Pulse Press, 2022

Contribute author of *Wounds I Healed* published by EIF, 2022

Contribute author of *Hidden in Childhood* published by Literary Revelations, 2023

Contribute author of *Heart's Desire* published by Prolific Pulse Press, 2023

Co-author of *A Collection of Paintings and Poetry of Australian Landscapes* published by Ark House, 2023

About the Author

CASSA BASSA is an Australian Chinese poet who lives in Sydney Australia. She started her English writing journey via  her blog *flickerofthoughts.com* where she writes poetry, prose, and micro stories.

She approaches life with deep thoughtfulness and imagination. Her focus in life is to help others to assist in changing their life for the better. She works with the disadvantaged people in the community, and she is constantly inspired by their strengths and resilience.

www.ingramcontent.com/pod-product-compliance
Lightning Source LLC
Chambersburg PA
CBHW050308260626
47156CB00005B/1711